W9-CBX-367

DO NOT RETURN IN JIFFY BAG

I DISCOVER COLUMBUS

I DISCOVER COLUMBUS

A True CHRONICLE *of the* GREAT ADMIRAL *& his* Finding of the NEW WORLD, narrated *by the Venerable Parrot* AURELIO, *who Shared in the* GLORIOUS VENTURE. *Set Down & Illustrated by* Robert Lawson

BOSTON

LITTLE, BROWN and COMPANY

Copyright 1941 by Robert Lawson
Copyright © renewed 1969 by Nina Forbes Bowman

All rights reserved. No part of this book may be reproduced in any form or by any
electronic or mechanical means, including information storage and retrieval systems,
without permission in writing from the publisher, except by a reviewer who may
quote brief passages in a review.

First Paperback Edition

ISBN 0-316-51760-7
Library of Congress Catalog Card Number 41-16483
Library of Congress Cataloging-in-Publication information is available.

10 9 8 7 6 5 4 3 2 1

BP

Published simultaneously in Canada
by Little, Brown & Company (Canada) Limited

Printed in the United States of America

j 970.01
L 485i

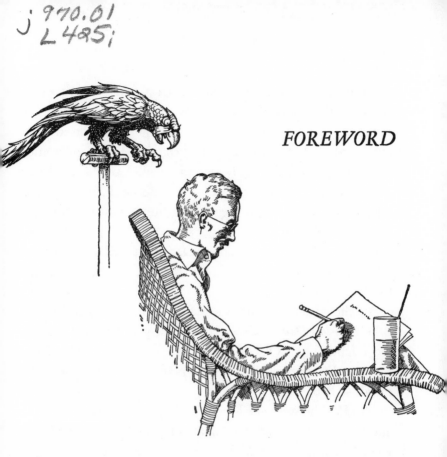

FOREWORD

THIS IS THE STORY told me by Aurelio, the old, old parrot of Don Tomás Francisco Glynn of Santa Margarita.

Santa Margarita lies upon the coast of Central America where the jungle meets the blue waters of the Caribbean and where nothing much ever happens nowadays, but a great deal went on in older times.

Once, recovering from a spell of tropical fever, I spent several weeks at the home of Don Tomás, resting and drowsing, as my strength slowly returned. My kind host was forced to be away a great deal of the time, so through the long quiet afternoons I lay upon the shady veranda, while Aurelio talked on and on, telling me the story of his life and deeds. It was a long tale, naturally, for it had been a long life: almost five hundred years, according to his calculations.

One afternoon the narrative was interrupted by sounds of celebration from the village; firecrackers, bands, shouts and the ringing of bells.

Aurelio glanced at the calendar and his crest rose in rage.

"Columbus Day!" he snorted. "Those poor ignorant peasants are celebrating 'COLUMBUS Day.' Columbus, 'The Great Explorer,' Columbus, 'The Great Navigator,' 'The Great Admiral' — Bah!

" 'Colón,' he was called in my day: plain Cristóbal Colón — and *I* could tell you what a 'Great Admiral' he was. *I* could tell you who *really* discovered the Americas, *I* could tell — "

"Why don't you?" I asked.

"I think I will," he rasped, ruffling all his feathers and settling on his perch. "I think I will; and see that you set it down correctly."

I know that some will question the accuracy of his story, but this they would never dare do if they were, as I was, face-to-face with Aurelio. There is a cold yellow gleam in those eyes, there is a keen curve to that huge beak, painfully like a pair of well-sharpened pruning shears, that somehow discourages any doubting of his word.

Rabbit Hill,
1940.

Robert Lawson.

CONTENTS

I DISCOVER COLUMBUS

· 1 ·

THE JUNGLE

IN THE YEAR 1491, said Aurelio, there was no happier parrot than I in all the jungles of Central America. In the full vigor of youth (I was then only about sixty-five years of age), surrounded by a numerous family and scores of gay companions, to me life seemed glowing and full of promise.

3

The jungle of those days was a very different place from that which you now know. No hunter's gun had ever shattered its peace, no ax had ever laid low one of its great trees. No steamboat ever disturbed the quiet surface of our slow-moving river nor polluted the fragrant air with the reek of its smoke.

The jungle Indians then were a sweet and peace-loving race, our dearest friends. We loved to ramble about their villages, joining in the children's games and talking gravely with the elders. They used to give us bits of their delicious toasted corn cakes, which they called *cracas,* and small pieces of sweet sugar cane to munch on.

We, in return, would cut for them the ripest fruits and nuts from high and inaccessible treetops and present them with our discarded tail feathers, which they prized highly as decorations. We would also carry messages to their friends and distant relations in other tribes scattered all over Central America. In this way I learned every different Indian dialect and I think it was this practice that later made it so easy for me to master Spanish and other languages and to become the accomplished linguist that I now am.

So in the steamy fragrance of the still, green jungle our lives flowed peacefully on until all this happy existence was, for me, rudely shattered by the terrible Hurricane of 1491.

There are a few parrots still living who can remember the awful fury of that storm. There still exists, in the upper reaches

4

of the Magdalena, an ancient alligator who could tell you breath-taking tales of the destruction it wrought.

But to me it came so suddenly that I scarcely knew what was happening or what strange changes it was to bring into my life.

· 2 ·

THE STORM

IT HAD BEEN frightfully hot all that day and the night brought no relief. In the lower branches where we usually roosted the air was like hot steam. This and the infernal racket of the thousand and one kinds of insects made sleep out of the question.

Seeking some cooler spot I had perched in the topmost bough of a majestic mahogany tree that towered high above the green roof of the jungle. Here the air was slightly better, but there was a heaviness in the atmosphere that bore down like a blanket and gave me a strange feeling of some coming terror. Far off, reddish lightning flickered and faint rumblings set all the leaves to trembling.

Finally I fell into an uneasy slumber.

I was waked from this by a terrific roaring of wind that sounded as though all the Great Mountains of the West had toppled from their bases and were tumbling across the country. Sheets of rain came so thick that I thought the gale must have lifted our river from its bed and hurled it through the air. Flashes of lightning showed the roof of the jungle tossing like a mad sea.

Then with a tearing crack the branch to which I clung was torn from its tree and whirled high in the air. Over and over, up and ever up, it flew — spinning like a dried leaf, while I tightened my roosting grip, closed my eyes and tried to hold on.

I was up high now; the crashing and tearing of the jungle had all ceased; there was only the roaring of the wind hurling me and my branch through the black night. Hour after hour this went on, till finally a dim light began to glow in the sky directly ahead. Through the broken clouds I caught a glimpse of the rising sun.

"Eastward," I thought, "I am going eastward, toward the

rising sun!" And then came the horrid thought: "I must be well out over the Great Ocean."

No sooner had this occurred to me than far below, through a gap in the clouds, I saw dark tossing waves.

"Well, so ends Aurelio," I muttered.

To make matters worse the wind seemed to be slackening somewhat and my branch was slowly losing speed, dropping toward the earth, or rather, water.

Of course I *could* fly, as a last resort, but none of our family had ever been noted for long-distance flying; and what use were puny wings over the vast expanse of that Great Ocean which spread no one knew how far? So I uttered a short parrot prayer and held tight to the branch.

It was falling rapidly now, plunging down through the hurrying clouds; but so great had been our height, and so great was our speed, that it was many hours before I finally broke through and saw — oh, blessed sight — LAND!

· 3 ·

SPAIN

TO EYES used to the lush green of the tropics, this land to which I was descending looked strange and forbidding. All its surface was brown, dry and dusty. Great mountains were gashed and furrowed by dried-up watercourses. No green any-where, save a few sickly orchards; no great forest trees, no broad rivers — just rocks and baked soil. All told, an uninviting sight; but at least it was solid land and not ocean.

I was rapidly approaching the earth now and could see that my present course was going to deposit me and my branch in the only green spot of this desolate countryside.

A group of large buildings was surrounded by a high stone wall and all the area within this was filled with rich trees, lawns and gardens. I could see fruit on the trees, a welcome sight, and the gleam of water in little ponds and fountains.

Now I was very close to the earth. My branch gave one last lift that just cleared the wall, and I crashed down in a stone-paved courtyard.

I could see men running from every direction, attracted by the noise of my arrival — and what a terrifying sight they were! Dark hoods shadowed their faces and long flapping robes gave them the appearance of a flock of the great condors of our Western Mountains.

Terrified, I sprang into the shelter of a huge old orange tree that overspread the court.

The sight of my branch seemed to fill them with the greatest excitement, for evidently it came from a tree unknown to them. They gathered around examining it, smelling and chew-ing the leaves and all the time pushing, shouting and jabbering in some strange language that I could not understand.

At length, tiring of this racket, and being extremely hungry, I stepped to the end of a limb and addressed them in my best Indian.

"Could anyone tell me," I asked politely, "where I am, where I might get something to eat, and where I could take a good long rest?"

At the sound of my voice their excitement became twice as great as before. As they shrieked and leaped about in astonishment it began to dawn on me that these poor benighted creatures had never seen a bird that could talk!

"Well," I thought, "this might be a great advantage to me, if I could only speak their silly language."

Finally one fat one, who seemed to be a person of some authority, gathered his wits and began shouting orders at the others. One of these, his long robes flapping, dashed into a near-by building. Above the chatter of the expectant crowd I could hear again and again the word "Colón."

Almost at once the messenger reappeared, escorting the strangest-looking individual I had yet beheld in this strange land.

The first thing that struck me was his hair. I had never before seen a human with anything but black hair. His was a gleaming golden-red which, in the sunlight, was really dazzling. In addition his eyes, unlike any that I had ever seen, were brilliant blue in color.

His clothes were of many glaring hues, mostly red, but all

12

very much patched and frayed. A long cloak with a moth-eaten collar hung from his shoulders and as he walked a bent sword in a tattered scabbard clattered upon the stones of the courtyard.

About his neck were hung several brass chains from which dangled a whole collection of ornaments and medals of brass, tin and copper.

He bore himself with the greatest dignity as he shouldered a way through the chattering crowd. The dark-robed ones seemed to treat him with some respect, but I noticed that behind his back they grinned and winked, pointing to their foreheads just as our Indians did to indicate a person who did not have very good sense.

He listened solemnly as they showed him the mahogany branch, examined it and then confronted me.

"*Cracas*," I said hopefully, for I was very hungry by now.

Apparently he did not understand, for he addressed me in the same speech that the Dark Robes used. Seeing I could not understand that he tried various other languages, all unfamiliar to me. I then spoke to him in every Indian dialect that I knew but to all of them he merely shook his head.

Finally I remembered the name the crowd had repeated so often.

"Colón," I said.

The effect was astonishing. "Colón!" he shouted, "Colón!

Colón!" and, pointing to his chest: "Colón, Don Cristóbal Colón!"

"Don Cristóbal Colón," I repeated dutifully, and the crowd broke out in shrieks of wonder.

"*Cracas?*" I suggested again, hopping to his shoulder, but again he looked blank, and I got hungrier.

With me still seated on his shoulder Don Cristóbal pushed his way through the wondering Dark Robes and entering the building, ascended a long stairway to what was apparently his room. A small fire in the fireplace made it warm and cozy, but what interested me most was the sight of a meal laid out on the table. There was a pitcher of milk and a plate of those small toasted cakes I was so fond of.

"*Craca,*" I exclaimed, helping myself to one.

Don Cristóbal looked on with interest. He pointed to the plate and asked, "*Cracas?*"

"Yes, *cracas,*" I said, and ate another.

Then he pointed to his chest again.

"Don Cristóbal Colón," I said promptly. He was vastly pleased and made me repeat it several times. Pointing to myself I said, "Aurelio."

"Aurelio," he repeated, "Aurelio."

It was in this manner that I began to learn Spanish and to teach him the speech of the Indians. For many long weeks I lived here in the room of Don Cristóbal. All day and far into the evenings we exchanged language lessons while he sewed and patched his already much-patched clothes or polished his gaudy decorations.

Before long we were able to converse with perfect freedom and I began to learn something about him and about this strange land to which I had been blown.

· 4 ·

FROM RAGS TO PATCHES

DON CRISTÓBAL COLÓN (or "Chris," as he now allowed
me to address him in private) had been born in Genoa, the son
of a poor weaver. He spent a most unhappy childhood toiling
at his father's looms and dye-vats.

Sometimes he was sent to deliver rolls of cloth to the palaces of the wealthy Genoese and the glimpses of luxury that he caught on these rare occasions had made him thoroughly discontented with his own poor lot. In fact he brooded so much about it that he became, I always thought, a little touched in the head. Of course he would never admit this, but he did tell me of the long days of labor in the steam of the dye-vats, of the endless monotony of the looms, and how all this had eaten into his proud and ambitious soul.

At an early age, he said, he had made a solemn vow that some day he would have finer clothes, richer jewels, grander palaces, and more high-sounding titles than any nobleman of the land. He had spent his entire life attempting to make these visions come true, so far with no success at all. For years he had wandered over most of the countries of Europe seeking honors and wealth at one court after another, always unsuccessful, always mocked and jeered at, usually hungry. At last, penniless, weary and ill, he arrived at the Convent of La Rábida, where the kindly monks took pity on him and nursed him back to health.

Shut off as they were from the outside world, they enjoyed his tall tales of all that he had seen and done at the great Courts. In return they humored his delusions, treating him with the utmost deference and always addressing him by the ridiculous titles he had bestowed upon himself. They furnished him with scraps of rich velvets and laces from worn-out altar cloths, and bits of brass and tinsel from broken church ornaments. It was from

17

these he had concocted his fantastic costumes and decorations.

He really should have been quite happy and contented there, but the old ambitions still burned brightly within him. As the effects of his recent illness wore off I could see that he was daily growing more restless and eager to be off again on his fruitless search for honors and fortune.

As for me, I was more than restless. I was completely miserable in this strange, harsh country, so different from the soft steamy warmth of my native jungle. The glaring sunlight hurt my eyes, the dryness cracked my skin, the sour, shriveled fruit gave me poor nourishment. I was growing thin, my plumage was losing its color. The nights were always cold and I had to crouch over the fire to keep halfway warm. It was unbearable.

I *must* get home, I resolved, I *must,* somehow. I can't last long in this miserable place. Somehow I must accomplish it!

But how? Between me and home there lay those hundreds, perhaps thousands of leagues of the Great Ocean. Day and night I pondered the problem and then, as I had almost despaired, a ray of hope suddenly appeared.

It all came about through a chance remark I made while telling Chris about my country. I happened to mention gold and at the word he started as though stung by a scorpion.

"Gold!" he shouted, "GOLD! Are there gold mines in your country?"

"What are mines?" I asked.

"Why, deep holes in the ground. Men go down on ladders to toil all day in the darkness and bring up small baskets of rock containing specks of gold."

"What a silly way of doing things," I laughed. "No, in my country we have no 'mines.' The gold there lies along the river banks and the men just pick it up in lumps."

"And silver?" he gasped, his eyes popping. "Is there silver? Are there pearls?"

"Of course there is silver," I answered impatiently. "It's so common that no one pays any attention to it. As for pearls, the Indian children play marbles with them."

"Marbles!" Chris exclaimed. "You don't say. Are there pearls big enough for that?"

"Big enough? Why they're *too* big, mostly. The children pick out the smallest ones for marbles and throw the others away."

He seemed stunned with wonder, and as he sat there a Great Idea came to me. A plan that might make it possible for me to get home again!

"Chris," I said suddenly, "you Spaniards seem to lay great value on gold and silver and pearls; why, I don't know, but you do. Now wouldn't your King and Queen, the Most Illustrious Ferdinand and Isabella, be awfully glad to discover my country, where all these treasures abound?"

"Would they?" exclaimed Chris, still in a daze. "WOULD THEY? Why they would — "

"All right," I interrupted. "Let us discover it for them."

"But how?" he asked weakly.

"Here's how," I said. "Now listen carefully, here is my plan. First you will draw some very pretty maps of my country, showing where the gold, silver and pearls lie. I can describe it to you, I've flown over it many times. Then you will write out the sailing directions for getting there. You can do that, can't you? You claim to be a great navigator?"

"Indeed yes," he exclaimed excitedly. "As a navigator there is not my equal in all Spain, in all the world perhaps. I can box the compass, shoot the sun, figure latitude and longitude, draw maps — beautiful maps — and handle an astrolabe as skillfully as any man — in theory, of course."

"Splendid," I said. "Now just get to work, and as soon as you are ready we will go to Court and tell the King and Queen about the wealth to be found in my country. . . .

"If they are as eager for gold as you say, they will gladly give us two or three ships to go and fetch it. They will probably make you an Admiral, with a cloak and medals. Then think of the welcome, when you come sailing back with a couple of shiploads of gold and silver. Think what the King will say when you give him a bag of pearls to play marbles with! Think of the honors! Think of the clothes!"

"I *am* thinking of them," he said; "but how, Aurelio, are we, two penniless adventurers, going to secure an audience with Ferdinand and Isabella, the greatest and most powerful rulers in Christendom?"

"You forget *me*," I said. "Haven't you noticed what a sensation I, Aurelio, the Bird-That-Talks, have made in this stupid country of yours? Why there hasn't been a day that the monks here haven't brought in dozens of people from miles around to see and hear me. Once the fame of my accomplishments has reached Their Majesties' ears they will *demand* our presence at court."

"True, true," murmured Chris, "I hadn't thought of that. I was thinking of my titles and honors — and a crimson cloak."

"Well, think of your maps," I said; "and see that you make them good."

Convinced now of the good sense of my plan, he went at his map making with the greatest enthusiasm. Within a few days he had drawn several very beautiful ones: the mountains of my land all glittering with gold, and the Great Ocean filled with sea serpents, whales and other terrifying creatures. He had also filled a whole book with sailing directions which looked very impressive.

When we informed the good monks of our coming departure they all set to most kindly to help with the necessary preparations. The Abbot contributed a lovely altar-hanging of purple velvet (practically new except where the rats had gotten at one end of it) and this Chris promptly made into a really striking cloak.

They polished his medals and gewgaws, stitched up his scabbard and even managed to straighten his sword pretty well, so that he finally presented a fairly respectable figure. Their last kind deed was to give him a mule to ride. It was not the handsomest mule I have ever seen, but it was good-natured and willing.

Everything at last being ready, we prepared to start out bright and early the next morning to seek our fortunes at the great Court of Ferdinand and Isabella.

· 5 ·

JOURNEY ON EGGS

SO WE BADE FAREWELL to the kind monks of La Rábida
and set forth on our journey. Mounted on the mule and wrapped
in his new purple cloak, Chris presented a very colorful figure,

whose dignity was only slightly marred by a large market-basket filled with food and wine which he carried on his arm. It was a comforting thought, however, for we had not a maravedi between us and were facing a trip of almost two hundred miles to Granada where the Court lay.

It was a beautiful summer morning and now that he was in action again Chris's spirits rose with every mile. The intense gloom which usually surrounded him blew away with the fresh breeze, we sang and whistled duets, he waved his sword or doffed his hat to each passer-by, and our adventure seemed to have started most happily.

We had a delightful lunch from the good monks' lavish basket and progressed thus contentedly until evening. As the chill twilight came I wondered what we should do about our night's lodging, but Chris reassured me with a gay laugh.

"Leave that to me, Aurelio," he shouted, "I am an old campaigner. I have travelled all the countries of Europe without a sol in my pocket, without a fine mule, or a lunch basket or a talented companion like you. Why, this is easy."

So saying he rode noisily into the courtyard of the best inn of the town that we were passing through and shouted loudly for service. He turned over our mule to the gaping stable boys, with orders that it be given the best of food and care, then strode into the common-room rattling his sword and demanding the innkeeper. The host, beholding this strange figure, bedecked in

24

his ridiculous garments, still carrying the lunch basket and with me perched on his shoulder, evidently decided that here was some eccentric nobleman, for we were promptly shown to the best room in the house and a lavish dinner was soon spread before us.

In the morning, as we ate our breakfast in the common-room, Chris talked very loudly of his exploits in the various Courts of Europe.

"This medal," he said, fingering one of his brass ornaments, "was given to me by the King of Sardinia for my extreme cleverness in making an egg stand on its end."

"But, Your Honor," exclaimed the hovering innkeeper, "such a thing is impossible! An egg *cannot* be stood upon its end."

"That's what the King of Sardinia thought," said Chris. "Would you care to make a small bet on it?"

"I am a poor man, Your Excellency," protested the landlord, "yet I would swear that it could not be done. I would even wager on it, had I anything to wager."

"Well, you might wager our bill for the night's lodging," said Chris kindly.

"But against what," asked the worried innkeeper, "suppose you lose?"

"In that case," said Chris grandly, "should I by any chance fail, you would become possessed of this magnificent bird." And he pointed to me!

"It *is* a handsome creature," the landlord admitted, "but hardly equal in value to a night's lodging."

I could see that it was now time for me to speak up.

"A night's lodging!" I shouted in my best Castilian. "A night's lodging! Why, you poor ignorant clod, have you ever before heard of a bird who could *talk?* Have you ever encountered a bird who could *sing?*" and I rendered a few bars of a popular melody. "Have you ever known a bird who could *whistle* — like this?" and I let loose a perfect burst of my most tuneful trills.

The effect was magical. The innkeeper fell backward in astonishment, while the other guests crowded around with exclamations of admiration and wonder.

"The bet!" they shouted. "The egg, bring on the egg!"

An egg was brought and as Chris examined it carefully the spectators pressed closer.

"And now, Gentlemen," cried Chris, raising the egg. "Behold!" and he plunked it down on the table, just firmly enough so that the end was crushed in and it stood upright.

The assemblage burst out in roars of laughter. "He wins!" they shouted. "He wins, it stands on end!"

"But, Your Highness," protested the innkeeper, "you have broken the shell."

"Did I say anything about the shell?" asked Chris. "Come, Aurelio, this is becoming tiresome and Their Majesties await us."

He swirled the purple cape about him, picked up the market basket, and amid the delighted laughter of the throng we took our departure.

In this manner our progress continued all the way to Granada. Word of my accomplishments sped before us, and each night we found our inn crowded with the curious, eager to see "the Bird-That-Talks." All the innkeepers were perfectly willing to be imposed on by Chris's egg trick for the extra trade that our presence attracted.

Arrived finally at Granada we took up quarters at the finest inn the town afforded. Scarcely had we settled to our dinner than a most imposing personage shouldered his way through the crowded common-room shouting, "Make way for the King's Messenger!"

Marching up to our table he demanded, "Have I the honor of addressing the illustrious Don Cristóbal Colón?"

"You have," said Chris, "and a true honor it is."

"The owner of the fabulous Bird-That-Talks?"

"The same," Chris answered. "Speak to the gentleman, Aurelio."

"Good evening," I said, "very pleasant weather you have here."

The gentleman started back, then straightened his wig and recited: "Their-Supreme-Highnesses-King-Ferdinand-and-His-Illustrious-Consort-Queen-Isabella — Lords-Rulers-Regents-and-

Viceroys-of-Castile-Aragon-Leon-Seville-Majorca-Minorca-Cata-
lonia-Estramadura-Granada-and-Lands-and-Islands-beyond-the-
Seas — Command-Your-Immediate-Presence-at-their-Imperial-

Court-without-Delay-on-Pain-of-their-Royal-Displeasure — A-Coach-Awaits-You! — And-Don't-Forget-the-Bird."

"Thank you," said Chris, when this was finished. "Just a moment until I finish my custard and wash my face and hands."

As he gathered up his maps and brushed his clothes I couldn't resist saying: "I told you so, Chris. Didn't I say we'd get an audience?"

An ornate coach with six horses and several footmen awaited. We entered it and were soon clattering through the winding streets that led to the Royal Court.

· 6 ·

FERDINAND AND ISABELLA

AS OUR COACH lumbered along toward the Palace, I could see that poor Chris was in a very nervous state, and well he might be! Perhaps this audience would bring true all his dreams

31

and ambitions. Perhaps his long search for wealth and glory would this night be crowned by success!

As for myself, I felt no uneasiness. Who were these petty rulers to me? I who had visited the opulent Courts of the Aztec princes, who had sat upon the very shoulder of the Supreme Inca?

To one who had paced the gold-encrusted terraces of the great Palace of Tenochtitlan, this poor Spanish castle that we had now entered appeared most unimpressive, in fact quite shabby — and very cold.

"Don't be nervous, Chris," I said quietly, as we were ushered down a long damp passage. "Keep your head and let me do most of the talking — and *all* the thinking."

We entered a great hall crowded with brightly costumed people and were announced by a Major-Domo as, "The Genoese, Cristóbal Colón — and bird."

The King and Queen sat at a long table strewn with the remains of a banquet and as the throng opened to allow our approach I had a good chance to observe them. I didn't care for Ferdinand's looks at all; he looked mean. Mean and coarse, and a little stupid. A man of action, perhaps, but very uncouth.

I decided at once that we must direct all our efforts at the Queen. While Isabella could hardly have been called pretty, she did seem intelligent and rather kindly as she smiled on

Chris and me. When we reached their table Chris swept off his hat with a flourish, made a deep bow that almost unseated me from his shoulder, and remained kneeling.

"Get up, get up," the King ordered. "Let's see the bird. Make him talk."

I remained silent, while Chris explained most respectfully: "This remarkable bird, Your Majesty, comes from faraway lands bringing tidings of such great import that it seems fitting they should reach Your Majesties' ears alone. In privacy, I am sure, Sire, he will talk to great good purpose."

"Nonsense!" roared the King. "It's all a hoax. I don't believe he *can* talk!"

"Talk!" I cried indignantly, hopping to the back of the Queen's chair. "Talk I can, till the ears of the world tire of the sound of it. But at the moment song seems more appropriate." So saying I sang the opening bars of "*Che Palazzo Paloma,*" a popular Spanish serenade. One of the musicians took up the tune on his guitar and while the audience sat in open-mouthed astonishment I sang to the ear of the Queen, sang with all the warmth of feeling at my command. As the song ended, everyone burst out in involuntary applause. The Queen was delighted and even Ferdinand looked less unpleasant.

"What else can he do?" he demanded of Chris.

"Whistle," I said, without waiting for a reply, and burst into

33

a camp song that I had learned in one of the taverns. It was a rather vulgar song, but had a rollicking tune. Soon the King was pounding time on the table with his fork and even the Queen's foot tapped gently in unison.

Seeing that Ferdinand was now in a better humor, I said quietly in the Queen's ear: "Your gorgeous Highness, Don Cristóbal and I have information of the greatest importance to Your Majesties and the Kingdom of Spain. May we not speak in private?"

"Of course," she replied, graciously, and turning to the King, "Sire, I weary of this crowd."

"Get out!" Ferdinand shouted, waving at the courtiers, who reluctantly withdrew. Then when we were left alone, except for a few of Their Majesties' Councillors, he turned to Chris and demanded, "Well, what *is* all this news that you bring? Come, speak quickly, it's past my bedtime."

Chris gathered up his maps and was preparing to make a long speech when the King again interrupted him. "What is this egg trick that I have heard rumors of?" he asked. "It seems you do something with an egg?"

"A mere nothing, Sire," answered Chris, "a simple, childish feat with which to fool the ignorant. Of no importance compared to the world-shaking tidings we bring."

"Bother your tidings," Ferdinand shouted, "I want a trick! HO there, Steward, fetch an egg, fetch an egg!"

"I will gladly oblige Your Majesty," said Chris; "but I must warn you that it is a very slight thing: merely causing an egg to stand on its end."

"Stand on its end?" snorted the eldest Councillor. "Why, that is absurd; no egg can be stood upon its end!" And all the other Councillors echoed him with "Ridiculous," "Preposterous," "Silly," "Can't be done," and so forth.

"Of course it can't," grunted the King sulkily. "Told you he was an impostor. Here, here's your egg, now let's see you do it."

"It is very simple, Your Majesties and Gentlemen," said Chris, raising the egg high. "I merely do this, and . . ."

PLOP!

I have never known whether Chris was overeager or the egg was overaged, — probably both, — but when he plunked it down on the table it burst with a resounding pop, liberally splashing the King and Councillors with its evil-smelling contents.

King Ferdinand's rage was wonderful to behold! With one breath he roared for his bodyguard, his Councillors, his Steward, and his Queen. "Throw him out!" he raged, "exile him, banish him, bring me a towel, call my lawyer, call out the Guard!"

I flew after poor Chris, who was being hustled toward the door, and perching on his shoulder for a moment whispered, "To La Rábida, but go slowly, I will have you called back soon,

35

cheer up, wipe that egg off your chin and *don't* lose your maps."

Then I flew back to the Queen, who was mopping the still-fuming Ferdinand and trying to stifle her giggles.

"Too bad," I murmured, "too bad."

"The egg, you mean; indeed it was, much too bad. I shall speak to the Steward about it in the morning," Isabella smiled. "In the meantime, follow me to my apartment."

After the King had stamped off to bed I followed Isabella down many long corridors to her chambers. Here we were joined by a dozen ladies in waiting, and very lively young things they were, too. Of course they were all agog to see me and to hear me talk, sing and whistle. Urged on by their admiration and flattery, I really outdid myself; and the Queen had considerable trouble in shooing them off to bed.

When the last one had reluctantly departed the Queen settled herself in a comfortable chair, gave me a stool to roost on, set out a bowl of fairly good fruit, and sighed, "At last, my dear Aurelio, we are alone and quiet. Now tell me about this important news that you and your unfortunate friend bring."

· 7 ·

AURELIO AND ISABELLA

"MOST GRACIOUS MAJESTY," I began, "our news concerns a land that lies far beyond the seas. A land where gold and silver and precious stones are as abundant as the leaves upon the trees."

"Hah," the King snorted, "I think that many of your friend
will find themselves without a roof over their heads when w
get there. What about silver?"

"Oh, of course silver is much more common," I replied
"Being stronger and of less beauty than gold, it is used mostl
for kitchen utensils, cooking pots and things of that sort. Als
for doors and window shutters and in the larger cities fo
paving the principal streets."

Ferdinand's eyes glittered greedily as he shouted: "And
pearls — you say there are pearls?"

"Pearls, Your Majesty, are perhaps the most plentiful of all.
 I told Don Cristóbal, the children use the smaller ones for
bles and toss away the larger ones as useless. In some districts
arents have had to forbid this practice, as the larger pearls
ed about made walking quite difficult."

w all present were in a perfect fever of excitement.
 where *is* this egg-man Colón?" fumed Ferdinand.
sn't someone bring him back? Why does everyone sit
g nothing? This is important! Why did you let me
 Cabrera, go and find him! Call out the Guard!
! *Do* something!"

 has been done, Your Majesty," said Isabella,
stóbal Colón now awaits our pleasure in the
rtunate that *someone* around this court has a
, summon Don Cristóbal."

At the word "gold" Isabella's eyes sparkled with interest.
"GOLD?" she exclaimed. "Gold and silver? Where is this
land? How can it be reached? Why have we not been told of
it sooner?"

"It lies far to the West, Your Majesty, beyond all the leagues
of The Great Ocean, but how far no one knows — except Don
Cristóbal Colón. Just how to reach it no one knows — except
Don Cristóbal Colón. He has made the maps and sailing directions. *He* knows the way; yet at this very moment this unfortunate Don Cristóbal is tramping the roads of Spain, banished
from Your Majesty's Court — merely because of an egg."

The Queen's interest was now intense. "Go on, Aurelio, tell
me more of this land of yours — But one moment . . ." And she
pulled a bell-cord. To the servant who answered she said: "Send
Cabrera at once."

Hardly had I started to speak when Don Manuel Cabrera,
the King's Chamberlain, was announced. He was a most imposing gentleman, but Isabella stood in no awe of him.

"Cabrera," she said, sharply, "through the stupidity of this
Court the most valuable person in all Spain has been banished
and sent wandering the road, penniless and hungry. You remember Don Cristóbal Colón, the owner of this delightful and
intelligent bird, whose lack of skill with an egg roused the
King's anger this evening. This Don Cristóbal is now making
his way on mule back to the Convent of La Rábida, near Palos.

You will take a company of the Guard and bring him back to me. Search every inn and roadside, and do not fail."

She tossed a small purse of gold on the table. "Buy him some fitting clothes and have him here before noon tomorrow, when the Council meets. Do not disappoint me, Cabrera." She passed her finger across her neck in a quaint little gesture that she often used, and the Chamberlain left hastily.

"And now, dear Aurelio," she continued, settling back, "tell me more about this country of yours, tell me more about the gold and pearls."

So for long hours I talked about my native land; about the jungle and its fruits, about the Indians and their ways, but mostly about gold and silver and pearls. Of course I made a lot of this up, for although I knew that there was plenty of treasure there I had never paid much attention to it. But since treasure was the only thing she wanted to hear about, I felt I must oblige her, and oblige her I did. The more I told her the more excited she became, and it was long past midnight before she would allow me to stop and go to roost on the elaborate canopy above her bed.

The Council met at noon, and it was not a very encouraging group of faces. At Isabella's right sat a grim-faced priest, very different from the kindly monks of La Rábida. He, I learned,

was Torquemada, the Grand Inquisitor, an excellent person to avoid. The King was there, less grumpy than the last evening, but still far from pleasant. In addition there were several grave, bearded gentlemen, among them Don Manuel Cabrera, Don Luis Santangel the King's Treasurer, the Duke of Medina-Sidonia, and the Archbishop of Toledo. I sat on the back of the Queen's chair.

Queen Isabella lost no time in telling them about the y of my land, repeating all that I had told her the previous She also pointed out that due to the stupidity of a ce present Don Cristóbal Colón, the one man in all knew how to reach this land, had been b Court.

I could see that the moment she men Councillors were gripped by that sar these Spanish people showed wh "gold."

"Let the bird speak," Fer you — Is it true that in the river banks that it

"Perhaps not qu answered. "Sin with gold, it easy to ga

· 8 ·

CHRIS DEMANDS

THE QUEEN'S purse of gold had seemingly been well spent, for Chris's costume was fairly dazzling in its newness. A long crimson cloak edged with fur replaced the old altar-cloth, new

43

doublet and hose of orange silk took the place of the old patched ones, and he carried a hat of purple velvet ornamented with a green plume. Only the sword and his string of glittering brass medals remained the same.

The new clothes seemed to have changed Chris too. He was no longer timid or nervous, but strode into the hall with head held high and approached Their Majesties with great assurance.

"Well, come, come," said the King impatiently, "you've wasted enough of our time already. Tell us about this land of gold and silver. Where is it? How do we get there? Where are these maps of yours? Why haven't you started?"

Chris began to speak, but was cut short by the King. "You needn't describe it, the bird has told us enough. What we want to know is how to get there. Why don't you tell us? Why don't you say something?"

"If Your Majesty will permit — " Chris began again.

"Permit," roared the King. "Permit! You dare demand that I, the King, permit — "

"Oh, hush, Ferdinand," said Isabella, wearily. "Do let the poor man speak."

The King sulked, while Chris, looking gratefully at the Queen, began: —

"Your Royal Majesties, before revealing these great discoveries, I fear that certain rewards and promises must be agreed upon. I have spent most of a lifetime of study and labor upon

44

this project and it seems only fair that such devotion should be fittingly repaid. I may add that King John of Portugal has made me a very handsome offer, and His Highness King Charles of France is even now awaiting an interview with me."

"That is but just," the Queen said graciously. "You may rest assured, Don Cristóbal, that we will not fail to be properly grateful, and that we will show that gratitude in a very practical way."

"All right, all right," grumbled Ferdinand. "What do you want? Come, name your price."

My heart sank as Chris unrolled a long scroll of parchment. Alas! I thought, these new clothes have given him an exaggerated idea of his importance. As he began to read the long list of his demands the hope of ever again seeing my dear jungle started to fade, and the more he read the more it faded.

"Firstly," he said loudly, "I shall be made ADMIRAL OF THE OCEAN SEA. As such I shall hold higher rank than any Admiral of any nation on any sea. This title to descend to my offspring, heirs and assigns throughout the ages."

Ferdinand started up in rage, but Don Luis Santangel whispered in his ear: "It is a mere empty title, Sire. Let him have it if he wants it. It won't cost us anything." The King sank back, glowering.

"Secondly," Chris went on, "I shall be Governor General of all these lands, when they are discovered."

"When and *if*," granted Ferdinand. "Go on, what more can you think of?"

"Thirdly, I, Don Cristóbal Colón, shall be made a Nobleman of Spain — with a coat of arms. Fourthly, I shall have one tenth of all the trade with these new lands. Fifthly, I shall have one eighth of all treasure, gold, silver or precious stones found in these lands. Sixthly — "

But the King could stand no more and even Isabella and the Council seemed astonished at these ridiculous demands.

"Throw him out!" Ferdinand suddenly roared. "Banish him! Exile him! Give him to Torquemada! The man is mad!"

Desperately I flew to the King's shoulder. "But, Sire," I whispered, "these are but promises — and promises are not *always* kept. Promise him anything *now,* but when once the land has been discovered and the ships come rolling home, laden with gold and pearls, then your Majesty *might* change your royal mind."

"Do you mean to suggest," he asked indignantly, "that I, Ferdinand, King of Spain, should make promises that will not be kept?"

"Exactly that," I answered.

"Bird," he said, "you have more sense than all my Councillors put together." Then, turning to Chris: "All right, all right, we agree. Let's have your contract, I'll sign it."

"But, Your Majesty, I have not finished, there are nineteen

more items," protested Chris, bewildered by this sudden change.

"Don't bother to read them," the King said. "They're granted. Here, give me the papers, give me a pen, give me some ink. *Why doesn't somebody give me something?*"

Then, while the Queen and Council sat in open-mouthed astonishment, he snatched the parchment, scrawled *Ferdinand Rex* across it, and tossed it to Isabella. As she signed, he turned again to Chris. "Very well, you are now ADMIRAL OF THE OCEAN SEA. Hope you enjoy it. When does our Expedition start?"

"Such an important undertaking will require a great deal of preparation, Sire," Chris answered, still in a daze. "A great deal of preparation — and a great deal of money."

"Very good," said the King shortly. "Get to work on it at once. Cabrera, find him a room. Santangel, find him some money. Isabella, come to dinner. Council is dismissed!"

· 9 ·

ADMIRAL OF THE OCEAN SEA

I HAD to spend the whole evening telling stories of the wealth of my land to the Queen and her ladies in waiting. Isabella never tired of hearing tales about the gold and gems, so I made up several good new ones.

The young ladies seemed to enjoy scratching me behind the ears, stroking my brightly colored tail feathers or plying me with fruits and cakes, all of which I found not unpleasant — except the fruit. That, as usual in Spain, was terrible.

So popular did I make myself that it was again very late before the Queen could persuade the gay young ladies to seek their beds and allow her to take to her own. When she was well asleep, I flew quietly out the window and went to look up Chris. Spying only one lighted window, high in a north tower, I judged that to be his room, so I flew up and looked in.

He was working busily, surrounded by books, maps, scrolls and all sorts of instruments.

"Well, Chris," I said settling on his chair-back, "our plans seem to be working out famously. You're already an Admiral, the expedition is guaranteed, gold and pearls will soon be rolling into the laps of the King and Queen, and perhaps *I'll* see my home again. Perhaps I'll once more set bill in a bit of fruit that's fit to eat. I've *got* to, Chris. I can't stand much more of this country. We just *have* to make this Expedition a success."

Chris pushed away his maps and calculations. "Look, Aurelio, look," he said in a sort of hushed voice, and pointed to a parchment pinned to the wall. It was covered with writing, ribbons and seals.

"I'm looking," I said; "what is it?"

"My commission," he said, still awestruck. "My Royal Commission. ADMIRAL OF THE OCEAN SEA! Cabrera brought it to me. Some of the letters are even done in gold leaf. Think of it, Aurelio, 'Admiral of the Ocean Sea,' a position of honor that no one has ever held before!"

"How could they?" I said. "You've just made it up. . . .

"Now Chris," I went on, as he continued to sit and gaze at his commission, "just forget these titles for a while and concentrate on the Expedition; that's the important thing. How are your preparations coming on?"

"Very well indeed, Aurelio," he said, finally tearing his eyes away from the parchment, "very well indeed. I have listed the ships, stores, men and equipment that will be required. I have even arranged the ceremonies for the departure of the fleet, and for the landing in your country. By tomorrow I shall be ready to present my plans to Their Majesties. The whole thing is going to take an awful lot of money though."

"Nonsense," I replied. "What are a few gold pieces now compared to the whole shiploads of treasure that will come sailing back? Get on with your calculations, Chris. Good night, I'll see you in the morning."

We met at noon the next day, just the King and Queen, Santangel, Chris and I. Chris was laden with rolls of parchment, scrolls, maps, books, lists and nautical instruments.

Ferdinand, who seemed in a rare good humor, greeted him almost pleasantly.

"Well, Admiral," he shouted, "you look like a paperhanger

50

about to go to work. Hah, hah, hah! Let's see the maps. Let's see the sailing directions. Why don't you show us your calculations? Where are the plans? Come, come, show us something, *show us something!*"

Chris displayed his maps and tried to explain the sailing directions and calculations. They occupied several books and none of us could understand them at all, but they looked very convincing. Ferdinand and Isabella, however, were fascinated by the maps. They exclaimed with delight over the mountains and rivers shining with gold, the pictures of the silver-walled palaces of Tenochtitlan, and the strange birds and animals that dotted the land and sea.

"Good, good," exclaimed the King, all eagerness. "When do we start? What do you need? Where are your lists, Admiral?"

When Chris began to read the long lists of what would be required for the expedition I could see the enthusiasm of the King and Queen turn to worry, as they watched the ever lengthening face of the Treasurer, Don Luis Santangel.

Ferdinand suddenly cut short this reading. "Come, come," he said irritably, "never mind the sea-boots and salt meat and sailcloth. What is the whole thing going to cost? Can't you give us a summary, a general idea?"

Chris, after fumbling and calculating a while, announced: "This glorious venture, Your Majesties, will require but three ships and about one hundred and twenty men. The total cost will be only seventeen hundred gulden."

"*Only seventeen hundred gulden!*" moaned Santangel, and clasped his head. We all sat in an uncomfortable silence, which was finally broken by the King.

"How — er — does the Treasury stand, Santangel?"

"Stand, Your Highness, *stand*? It does not stand — it totters. As your Majesties well know, our war with the Moors has swept the Treasury completely clean. We have not enough to pay last month's meat bill. Only yesterday Cabrera was forced to let three cooks and twelve footmen go. I have six men probing the Treasury floors with toothpicks, but so far they have only unearthed a handful of coins, and those mostly coppers. *Seventeen hundred gulden!* As well ask for seventeen million! And shiploads of gold waiting for us!" He clasped his head tighter and the gloom grew deeper.

"What about the Duke of Medina-Sidonia?" asked the King. "Could we borrow a little, do you think?"

"Did Your Majesty note his doublet last evening?" answered the Treasurer hopelessly. "Patched! Patched, Sire, in two places. And last week he sold his state coach and two suits of armor. No, nothing there."

The gloom grew still deeper and mine was deepest of all.

Suddenly Isabella rose with a gesture of irritation.

"You men!" she exclaimed. "You helpless men!" And clapped her hands.

At the sound a door opened and half a dozen of the ladies

in waiting entered, all bearing caskets which they placed before the Queen and retired.

Isabella swept them open, tumbling their glittering contents upon the table. "Gentlemen," she announced, proudly, "my jewels!"

"Well, what about them?" the King inquired, rather stupidly.

"About them?" answered Isabella, impatiently. "Why, I shall pawn them, of course. We MUST have seventeen hundred gulden!"

"Preposterous!" shouted the King. "Impossible! Think what our neighbors would say. Why, if the news got about that Spain was this poor, Charles of France would have an army on our border within a week, Sicily would revolt, Portugal would attack us, the Moors would come back. No, no! It cannot be done!"

"Oh dear," sighed the Queen, "I hadn't thought of that. I suppose it can't." She sank back hopelessly.

The gloom again started to settle, but the sight of the jewels had given me an idea. Desperate lest our plans should all collapse, I realized that someone must take a firm hand.

"Your Majesties, and gentlemen," I said, "this is a trifling matter which I will be most glad to attend to myself. I can guarantee to pawn enough of these jewels to raise our funds without anyone's hearing a word of it. Rest easy, Your Majesties. Admiral, proceed with your preparations. Don Luis, set those men who are scratching cracks to building an addition to the treasury. Leave this affair to Aurelio."

"Well," said Ferdinand doubtfully, "I guess we'll have to, but it doesn't seem possible. Meeting's dismissed."

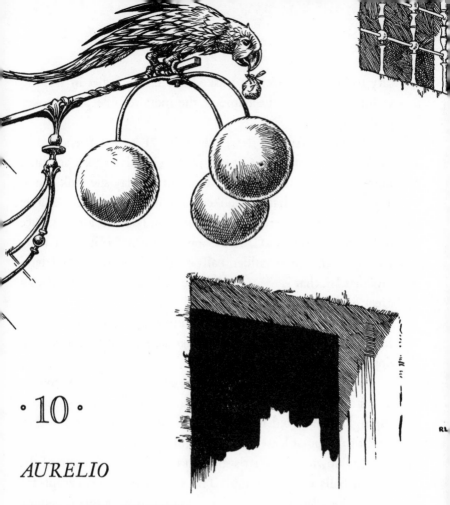

· 10 ·

AURELIO

THE ARRANGER

PAWNING THE JEWELS turned out to be a very simple
matter, much easier than I had dared hope. Since it was neces-

sary to keep strict secrecy I asked one of the ladies in waiting to find out for me the name of the most reliable pawnbroker in the city.

"Of course, Aurelio dear," she said. "I have a friend," and she blushed prettily, "a Captain in the Guards, who, I am sure, knows all about such things." Later in the day she took me to a broad window that overlooked most of the city. "The name, Aurelio," she whispered, "is Issachar, Don Issachar, and his place of business is on the Calle Lisbon. You can see it from here. Do you see the three golden balls over the doorway? My friend says that Issachar is the *least* dishonest of any. He himself does a great deal of business there, poor dear."

"Thank you, child," I said, gently nipping her little pink ear. "Any time you want a message carried or a little spying done, just call on old Aurelio."

That night I had the Queen place two magnificent diamonds in a small soft leather pouch. "Aren't they beauties, Aurelio?" she sighed. "An old beau of mine — well never mind — they ought to bring at least a hundred gulden apiece."

I flew down to Issachar's shop and perched on the sign of the golden balls to look around. The shop was empty, except for a tall, bearded man who was poring over a great ledger. I judged him to be Don Issachar. Walking in, I hopped up on his desk and spilled out the two diamonds on the ledger.

"How much?" I asked.

Issachar seemed slightly startled when he looked up and saw that a bird addressed him, but his real interest lay in the diamonds. He snatched them up, stuck a glass in his eye, and examined them with the greatest of care. Finally he tossed them back on the desk, picked up his pen and went back to his figuring.

57

"Fifteen gulden each," he muttered, "two for twenty-five."

"Too bad," I said, sadly, replacing the diamonds in their bag. "Too bad! I was told that Don Issachar knew something of the value of really fine stones."

"Twenty each," he said, without looking up.

I picked up the bag and started indignantly from the shop.

"Twenty-five each," said Issachar. I continued without even replying.

"Wait!" he shouted suddenly. As I paused he went on, "I can see that you know something about values. Well, how much do you want?"

"One hundred and fifty gulden each, and not a maravedi less," I replied firmly.

Don Issachar screamed and protested, he clasped his head and tore his beard, he squirmed and he moaned, but at last we settled on one hundred gulden apiece for the diamonds.

Once we were agreed I said, "Don Issachar, I have a proposition to make. Could you use more jewels like these?"

"Bushels," he said. "Why?"

"You have never had a bird as a partner, have you?" I asked.

"Certainly not," he answered. "Why should I? A bird — what an idea!"

"The greatest idea of the century," I said earnestly. "Do you realize that there are hundreds of wealthy nobles in this city? Do you realize that with true Spanish carelessness they leave jewels like these scattered over their dressing tables at all times?

Do you realize that at this season all windows are left wide open? Do you realize, Don Issachar, that a bird can fly into any window with the greatest of ease? Picking up a few of these baubles here and there is no more trouble to an intelligent bird than gathering a few grains of corn. And I, if I must say it, am a *very* intelligent bird."

As the pawnbroker slowly took in my meaning his eyes glittered with excitement. He extended his hand.

"Partners!" he exclaimed, "and *what* a partner! There's millions in it!"

It took me five trips to carry the two hundred gulden back to the palace. Isabella was delighted as I poured the shining gold pieces into a coffer. She already had two more diamonds sewed up in a pouch, ready to be pawned.

"Put them away, Your Majesty," I said, "just give me the bag." For my talk with Don Issachar had given me an idea.

In the next three weeks unnumbered jewels disappeared from the palaces of various grandees and somehow came to rest in the strongbox of Don Issachar in the Calle Lisbon. And each night I poured a new supply of gold pieces into Isabella's coffers.

The Queen could not understand it. "Aurelio," she said, in bewilderment, "where does all this gold come from? I thought you were going to pawn my jewels, yet you never take any of them."

"Why *yours*, Your Majesty," I answered, "when your subjects have so many, and are so careless with them?"

"But," she said, doubtfully, "I thought I had beggared all my people for the Moorish war. How can they have any jewels left?"

"They've been holding out on you, my dear," I said sleepily. "There are plenty more where these came from. Now do let's get some rest, I've had a busy evening."

Chris and Isabella, Cabrera and Santangel ran around day after day, buying ships and enlisting men, while I slept days and worked nights. They spent the gold almost as fast as I could bring it in, but at last they announced that all preparations were completed and at a cost of exactly seventeen hundred gulden. I had drawn over two thousand gulden out of Issachar, so the Queen had a few hundred left over for herself, and only two of her jewels had been pawned!

She was truly grateful and expressed her thanks on every occasion.

"Nonsense, Your Majesty," I said. "I'd do twice this for a good basket of mangoes. Now go buy yourself a new gown or two, you certainly do need them, those patched things you are wearing are disgraceful. And you might give a small present to that cute little thing who gave us the name of Issachar the pawnbroker."

Chris was simply beaming with happiness. "We have a

60

splendid fleet, Aurelio," he said. "Not what it should be, of course, for such a glorious venture, but it will do, it will do. We have three ships; the *Niña,* the *Pinta* and the *Santa María,* all a little worm-eaten but we got them cheap, very cheap. We have Captains, seamen, pilots, priests, a Grand Constable, a historian, a doctor; and you, Aurelio, will be the interpreter. All we need now is a Commander."

"A Commander?" I asked, bewildered. "Why Chris, aren't you the Commander?"

"No indeed, Aurelio," he answered, with a peculiar shifty expression. "No indeed. I have too much to attend to here in Spain. And then there is my position, you know. The Admiral of the Ocean Sea could hardly take personal command of such a small expedition." He went on and on, giving a hundred reasons why he could not go, while I sat in stunned silence.

"But, Chris," I protested, "the King and Queen expect you to lead this Expedition; everyone expects you to. This may wreck the whole affair."

For hours I tried to reason with him, but all in vain. With mulelike determination he refused to listen to my arguments. At length, weary and discouraged, I returned to the Queen's canopy and sought sleep.

· 11 ·

WANTED, ONE ADMIRAL

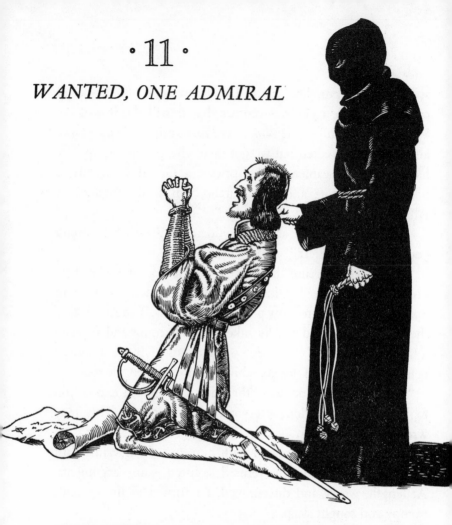

ONCE MORE the Council met and again the King seemed in a fairly good humor. He shouted, almost jovially, at Chris, "Well, well, well! I understand that everything is ready. Splendid work, splendid work. I am really pleased with you. When do you start? When do you start? Come now, come, no more delay, no more delay! When do you start?"

"We are indeed well prepared, Your Majesty," said Chris. "All that now remains is to select a leader for this glorious venture."

Everyone looked astonished and Ferdinand seemed thunderstruck.

"What, what, what?" he sputtered. "A leader? a leader? Why, *you're* the leader. What did we make you an Admiral for? Come, come, don't be silly, don't be silly!"

"Nay, Sire," answered Chris, pale but determined. "As Admiral of the Ocean Sea my rank is far too exalted to take personal command of such a small expedition. Three ships only! Why, any ordinary Admiral or Vice Admiral can take charge of that! My responsibilities are much greater. Why, Sire, this is just a beginning. There are whole fleets to be built; these three little ships cannot begin to bring back all the treasure that lies over there. There are docks to be constructed, warehouses for the gold and silver to be planned, new commanders to be appointed, new maps to be made. All this *I* must oversee. Nay, Sire, my place is here in Spain."

He really became quite eloquent and the King finally seemed convinced, but grumpy.

"All right," he growled, "all right, all right. Cabrera, go bring us a few Admirals to pick from. There ought to be plenty of them hanging around."

Cabrera reappeared almost at once with two or three Admirals, and went off looking for more.

The first of these to approach the Council table was Don Juan de la Sena, Admiral of Biscay and Teneriffe, a great, red-bearded giant of a man who looked as though he feared nothing on land or sea.

But when the plans and maps of the expedition were made plain to him he turned paler than Chris, if possible, and fell upon his knees before the King.

"But, Sire," he pleaded. "This is the Great Ocean, The Sea of Darkness, on which no man has ever dared to venture. Huge serpents and strange creatures infest it, the air is filled with loathsome birds. Terrible storms churn its waters. And somewhere out there one comes to the edge of the world where the Ocean pours down into black nothingness. Nay, nay, Your Majesties, anything, anything but that."

Ferdinand's look grew black. "You refuse?" he demanded. Don Juan de la Sena nodded.

"You would prefer a dungeon?" the King asked, icily.

"A thousand dungeons."

"Perhaps Torquemada and his little friends can reason with you," Ferdinand went on smoothly. "You are, perhaps, familiar with the Inquisitors and their ways? You would, no doubt, prefer to have your fingernails drawn slowly, one by one, with red-hot pincers, or to swallow little pellets of molten lead? You would, perhaps, enjoy a good stretch on the rack?"

64

"At least, Your Majesty," the Admiral cried, in desperation, "I shall die holy!"

"Holy or in parts," said Ferdinand, laughing grimly at his horrid joke.

Then, with an angry roar: "Take him away, Torquemada. he is yours. Next!"

"Next" was a mincing young man, gorgeously costumed, who advanced gracefully, kissed Isabella's hand, and knelt before the King.

"Can this be an *Admiral?*" Ferdinand grunted.

"Indeed, Sire, I am," the youth lisped, "but of course the title is purely honorary. Inherited, I believe, from my great-grandfather on my mother's side. I have never seen the sea, but I *have* designed some of the *loveliest* gowns for Her Majesty, haven't I, Your Majesty?"

"Take it away," groaned the King. "Don't even waste a dungeon on it, we'll need all of them, apparently. Who's next?"

The next came and the next, and the same thing went on for hours. A steady stream of Admirals and Vice Admirals appeared, but each one preferred the dungeon and the attentions of the grim-faced Torquemada to venturing upon this Sea of Darkness.

Finally Cabrera approached the King. "Alas, Your Majesty," he moaned, "that's all there are. Every Admiral or Vice Admiral of Spain is now in a dungeon or has taken to the hills. There aren't any more."

"Bah!" roared Ferdinand. "A fine lot of Admirals I have! A fine lot of expeditions I have! Glorious Ventures, bah! Council's dismissed! Bah! The whole thing's dismissed! Bah! Bah! Bah!"

And he stamped from the room.

· 12 ·

CAVALRY ADMIRAL

THE QUEEN and I sat in a deep gloom that evening. It would be hard to say whose gloom was deepest, but I think mine was.

"Well, I suppose I'll just have to learn to eat this awful Spanish fruit for the rest of my life and like it," I said despairingly. "I suppose I'll have to give up all hope of ever seeing my friends and family, of ever feeling comfortably warm nights, of ever — "

"My poor Aurelio," the Queen said, scratching my chin, "you have worked so hard, you have done so much, you have really been responsible for the whole expedition.

"Oh! those cowardly Admirals!" she burst out, her eyes flashing with anger. "They have ruined everything! I hope Torquemada is dealing with them as they deserve. And your Don Cristóbal, I think he is a coward too. All that talk about it being necessary for him to remain here! I think he is just afraid to go. Yet I cannot *force* the Admiral of the Ocean Sea to lead this venture, his rank is too high for that."

"I don't know *what's* the matter with him," I said hopelessly, "I just don't know. I don't think he's afraid of those sea serpents and things, he made most of them up himself. But ever since he got that commission and some new clothes he's been completely unreasonable. I just don't know *what* has gotten into him."

We sat in silence while the clock ticked and the gloom thickened. Then suddenly I had an idea.

"Listen, Your Majesty, I think I have it," I exclaimed. "We can't use force and we can't use reason, so we must use guile. Now here is the guile: —

"First we must find some ambitious young man who is not afraid of the Sea of Darkness. Some young soldier, say, who has never been near the water or heard these sailors' old wives' tales. You will make him an Admiral, a very temporary Admiral, and he will volunteer to lead the Expedition. Can that be done?"

"Easily," said the Queen, eagerly. "Go on, Aurelio."

"Now, Don Cristóbal has arranged a very elaborate ceremony for the departure of the fleet. There will be Your Majesties and most of the Court, Church dignitaries, musicians, salutes and, of course, the Admiral of the Ocean Sea himself, in a brand-new costume.

"My plan is simply this. Once aboard, our false Commander will induce the Admiral to come to his cabin and talk over last-minute instructions. While they are engaged in this the captains of the ships will quietly loose their moorings, raise a sail or two, and the expedition will be off, with the Admiral of the Ocean Sea in command, whether he likes it or not!"

"Aurelio, my jewel!" Isabella exclaimed, as I finished. "What a scheme! What a mind! How I wish you were a man!"

"How I wish *you* were a parrot," I answered gallantly, "but you're not, so let's get to work; we have plenty to do. . . .

"Now for our young man," I began, "our spurious Admiral. What about this Captain of the Guards, the friend of your cute little lady in waiting, Doña What's-her-name, who was so helpful in the affair of Don Issachar?"

"The very man," said Isabella, delightedly. "You seem to read

69

my thoughts, Aurelio. I know him well. He is young, brave, and ambitious. Very much in love and very much in debt. He has never seen a ship or heard of the Sea of Darkness. A perfect Spanish Admiral. . . !

"The lady you speak of is Doña María Mercedes d'Acosta. I will send her for the Captain at once."

While we waited for them I went on outlining my plans. "We should have a meeting of the Council tomorrow to confirm the new Admiral. The day after that, we must arrange matters with the Captains of the ships. The next day, the Expedition *should* sail. Only three more days, Your Majesty!"

Doña María Mercedes d'Acosta soon returned, leading her young Captain. He seemed to be all that Isabella had described, altogether a most gay and attractive young man.

"Have you no fear of the Sea of Darkness?" I asked him.

"Never heard of it," he laughed, "but I'm sure it couldn't be half so terrifying as my creditors."

The Queen told him carefully the part he was to play. It seemed to appeal to his adventurous spirit, for when she had finished he knelt before her to kiss her finger-tips.

"I will undertake with the greatest joy to carry out Your Gracious Majesty's wishes to the letter," he assured her.

"You realize that you must make the whole voyage?" the Queen asked. "It is a long and perhaps dangerous one."

At this Doña Mercedes grew pale and her dark eyes grew larger.

"But oh, Your Majesty," she murmured, "it will be *so* long, months and months."

"Nonsense, child," I said. "What are a few months? Only think, he will come home soon with bushels of gold for you and perhaps a hat full of pearls."

"He will also come home a Colonel," said the Queen; "a Colonel of the Royal Guards."

The young Captain bowed deeply to hide his joyous eagerness, but in the eyes of Doña Mercedes were only unhappiness and tears.

When the Council met the next morning our gay young Captain appeared, resplendent in the scarlet cloak of an Admiral of Spain.

"What's this, what's this?" sputtered Ferdinand. "Don't tell me we have an Admiral who's willing to make this journey? Don't tell me. I can't believe it. I can't believe it! Who is this young man, who is he? Never heard of him. Who is he? Why doesn't someone tell me who he is?"

"Admiral Don Manuel Nicosa, Your Majesty," answered Isabella, smoothly. "Not only willing, but eager to lead this glorious venture, for the profit and glory of Spain."

"Excellent, excellent!" exclaimed the King. "Fine spirit. Young blood — just what we need. Spirit of youth and all that. Splendid! Splendid! When does he start?"

"With Your Majesties' kind permission," I answered, "the Expedition will sail from the port of Palos on August third; that's the day after tomorrow. Admiral Don Cristóbal Colón has arranged appropriate ceremonies."

"Fine, fine," said Ferdinand. "We'll be there. Everyone will be there. Of course, of course. Council's dismissed."

· 13 ·

WE'RE OFF!

ON THE MORNING of August third, 1492, a gay and brilliant procession wound down the hill to the docks of Palos.

In the lead rode a company of the Royal Guards. Behind them came scores of gorgeously robed Church dignitaries accompanied by a host of censer-swinging altar boys. These were followed by a great choir singing Te Deums, more altar boys, and then Their Royal Majesties, the King and Queen of Spain.

At their right hand, mounted on a handsome white mule and dazzlingly costumed, rode the Admiral of the Ocean Sea, Don Cristóbal Colón. Behind us came a company of musicians and after them trooped the entire Court. Coach after coach, filled with bevies of laughing ladies, was escorted by most of the knights and grandees of Spain, superbly mounted and magnificently arrayed. There was, however, a noticeable absence of Admirals.

Seated on Chris's shoulder I could look back and see the whole length of this colorful throng, gleaming with gold and brilliant jewels, as it moved slowly down the winding road. Ahead and below us lay the little town of Palos, with its red-roofed buildings and its deep blue harbor. Tied snugly to its pier lay the three tiny ships of our expedition, the *Niña,* the *Pinta* and the *Santa María.*

To Chris this represented the climax of a life of toil and privation, the answer to all his dreams. He seemed a little dazed with pride and happiness as he nodded gravely to the cheering crowds which lined our way.

As for myself, I had too much on my mind to pay any great attention to the festivities. Hastily I thought over all that Isabella and I had done the day before.

We had rehearsed our young cavalry Admiral until he knew

his part perfectly. We had interviewed the Captains of the three ships. We had told them of our plans for the departure. We had impressed them with the importance of loosing their mooring lines quietly at my signal and dropping away from the pier with the least possible confusion.

As an extra precaution the Queen had used her quaint little gesture of the finger drawn lightly across the throat.

"There will be no mistakes, gentlemen," she warned gently.

The Captains, sweating slightly, assured her that there would be none.

There were a thousand other details to attend to and it was midnight before Isabella had time to bid me farewell.

"I will say good-by now, dear Aurelio," she said, "there will be no opportunity tomorrow. You have been a true friend and I shall miss you sorely. Think of us when you are home in your beloved jungle." She held my claw for a moment and then hung a small locket about my neck. On it was engraved *Remember Isabella*.

Arrived at Palos, the cavalcade spread out over the pier and swarmed upon the decks of our three ships. The choir sang and the musicians played, while the Church dignitaries began their long ceremony of blessing the Expedition.

Our young Admiral Manuel Nicosa was playing his part excellently. As he dashed around shouting orders and then countermanding them, he gave a splendid imitation of a busy commander. I joined Chris and Their Majesties, who stood on the quarter-deck of the *Santa María,* surrounded by a group of courtiers. I was relieved to see that two alert seamen stood by each mooring line and that Juan de la Cosa, our navigator, watched them like a hawk.

The priests had by now blessed the Expedition, the officers, the crews and the ships. They had blessed the sails, the food, the banners, the spars, and were now starting on the anchors. Realizing that this was almost the end of their ceremony I motioned to young Manuel Nicosa, who immediately joined the group on the quarter-deck.

"Your Excellency Admiral Colón," he said, after apologizing to Their Majesties, "there are just a few points in the sailing directions that I should like to go over with Your Excellency before we sail. If Your Excellency would be so kind as to step down to my cabin for a moment?"

Chris hated to miss any of the festivities, but as he hesitated the Queen said, "By all means, dear Admiral, leave no smallest detail in doubt. No mistakes must mar this glorious venture." As she smiled sweetly her finger idly traced the thin line of a golden chain that encircled her throat. Chris went below.

The moment he disappeared she grasped Ferdinand's arm and started him toward the gangplank.

"What — what — what?" the King sputtered. "Where — why — "

"Hush!" hissed Isabella. "Ashore at once, quietly. Don't ask silly questions and *don't* trip over that rope!"

At a gesture from her the courtiers tiptoed softly ashore. A glance assured me that the decks of the *Niña* and *Pinta* had been cleared of visitors. The seamen stood by their hawsers and the three captains watched tensely for my signal.

I hopped to a skylight that looked into the great stern cabin. Chris and Manuel Nicosa were deep in discussion over a pile of charts.

Stretching to full height, I spread wide my wings and waved them slowly up and down. At this signal the seamen, quick and silent as cats, loosed their mooring lines. The outgoing tide gently grasped us, the pier began to slide slowly past — and we were off!

Quickly I called down the skylight: "Plenty of time, Chris, the King is just about to begin his speech."

It was a fortunate thought, for the crowd, seeing our ships in motion, set up a great cheer, the musicians played, cannon boomed, church bells rang and the choir burst into a loud chant.

"The King, I suppose?" said Chris, intent on his maps. "My speech is next, isn't it, Aurelio?"

"Yes, Chris," I answered, "but it'll be a long, long time before your turn comes."

The swift, smooth-running tide had now carried us far down the harbor. The white walls of Palos were shrinking in the distance when I again signaled Juan de la Cosa. At once his soft-footed seamen loosed two small sails. A gentle breeze filled them and our speed increased.

As we neared the harbor mouth I hopped down to the cabin, where Chris and our young Captain-Admiral were still studying the charts.

At this moment the *Santa María* met the first long ocean swell. She rolled perceptibly.

A pale greenish gray pallor overspread Chris's countenance. He staggered to his feet and like a blind man groped his way to the cabin window. As his glazing eyes took in the distant towers of Palos, and the *Niña* and *Pinta* under full sail off our beam, he uttered a choking cry of despair.

"Betrayed!" he moaned. "Betray — awa-a-a-eugh — "

Those were the last words he spoke for several days. We helped him to his berth and called the steward.

He was seasick! Don Cristóbal Colón, the Admiral of the

81

Ocean Sea, was the seasickest person who ever lived! Now I realized why he had protested and hesitated. Now I knew why he had thought up all those reasons for remaining in Spain!

"So *that* was it," I said to Manuel Nicosa; "so *that* was why he could not take command. Well, our great Expedition seems to have two great Admirals, one of them seasick and the other a cavalryman. It's fortunate that we have Aurelio."

· 14 ·

THE GLORIOUS VENTURE

THE JOURNALS and diaries of Admiral Don Cristóbal
Colón tell that this great voyage was one long series of storms,

privation and perils. I must say that I think the perils were mostly in his mind and the storms in his middle. For to me it all seemed a joyous and rollicking adventure.

We had left Palos far astern, and with a pleasant breeze were rolling along to the westward, when Juan de la Cosa came to report to the Admiral. Glancing doubtfully at Chris's limp form, he asked:

"To which Admiral do I report?"

"To me, I suppose," Manuel Nicosa answered, laughingly. "But you know perfectly well that I'm no more an Admiral than you are a hummingbird. Here are the charts and sailing directions, which you probably understand, I certainly don't. You Captains will just have to get along as well as you can until he recovers."

"Heaven be praised," said De la Cosa, devoutly. "This will be the first expedition I have ever undertaken that didn't have an Admiral upsetting things. The orders are simple, just sail toward the setting sun until we get somewhere. A thousand thanks, Your Excellency. Have no fear, we will take care of everything." He departed happily, clutching his charts.

"Well, Aurelio," grinned Admiral Nicosa, cocking his feet up on a stool, "our Glorious Venture seems to have begun well. And by the way, would you mind calling me 'Nick'? I can't get used to this 'Admiral' and 'Your Excellency' thing."

The gentle motion of the ship, the soft breeze that fluttered the cabin curtains, the dancing light reflected from the waves, all suggested a nap to me. After all, I had had a rather hard three weeks. We had both started to doze when De la Cosa again appeared.

"A thousand pardons, Your Excellency," he said, "but we have just discovered a stowaway. He seems a very delicate youth; we can never make a sailor of him. What are Your Excellency's orders?"

"Bring him in," said Nick sleepily. "let's see him." Two sailors thrust a slender, pale-faced boy into the cabin.

"Well, well," demanded Nick, gruffly, "who are you? How did you get aboard? What do you want? Come, come; speak up, my lad, speak up."

The youth made an effort to speak, but no words came. His dark eyes filled with tears, and then suddenly — *"Mercedes!"* shouted Nick.

I rushed the bewildered Juan de la Cosa up on deck. "Captain," I explained, "your stowaway seems to be the Doña María Mercedes d'Acosta, Lady in Waiting to Her Majesty the Queen, niece of the Duke of Medina-Sidonia, ward of the Archbishop of Toledo — "

"Jesús!" exclaimed the Captain. "I almost had him — her — whipped!"

That night we had a wedding, the first, I believe, that ever took place on the Sea of Darkness. (I cannot imagine why this beautiful ocean was ever given such a sinister name.) The breeze had dropped and our three little ships lay peacefully, under the light of a golden August moon.

Small boats brought guests from the *Niña* and the *Pinta*. The good priest Gonsalvo Gomez was present to perform the ceremony. The Grand Constable was there, as well as the Captains and Pilots of all the fleet: Martin Alonzo Pinzon, Francisco and

Vicente Yañez Pinzon, and Pedro Alonzo Niño. Every seaman who owned and could play a musical instrument was brought along.

Doña Mercedes, who had concealed a bundle of feminine clothing when she slipped aboard, was now dressed suitably, while Manuel Nicosa in his crimson Admiral's cape made a gay and handsome bridegroom. Our Captain, Juan de la Cosa, insisted that it was his privilege to give the bride away. "Who has a better right?" he laughed, jovially. "My men found her, and findings is keepings."

The only important personage absent was the Admiral of the Ocean Sea. Poor Chris still lay in his berth, a gray-faced figure of misery.

An extra ration of wine was served to all the crews, and as the wedding ceremony ended the guns of the fleet boomed out an Admiral's salute, ship's bells were rung and the musicians burst into melody. The festivities continued far into the night.

Our voyage, thus happily begun, went on in the same spirit through the weeks of August and September. I have always felt that this was due entirely to the fortunate presence of Doña Mercedes, for she spread a gay kindliness through all the fleet, without which, I am sure, the whole expedition would have been a failure.

She was busy from dawn to dusk. She chatted with the sail-

ors, she ministered to the sick, she darned and mended, laughed and sang. When the weather permitted she was rowed to the *Niña* and the *Pinta* to visit their homesick crews. She went into the galleys and talked with the cooks, whereupon the food became almost edible. She borrowed a guitar and to its accompaniment sang the old ballads of Leon and Castile, of Aragon and Granada, while the mariners sat in open-mouthed admiration.

She even worked on Chris and his seasickness. She wrote his journal and diary for him, at his dictation. She opened the windows and let the fresh air blow through his cabin, which was a relief to everyone. She encouraged him to eat, she chatted to him by the hour of the riches that awaited us and the glory and honors that would be his on returning to Spain.

So well did she accomplish her task that after a few weeks he was sitting up and taking a little nourishment, and toward the end of September he actually ventured on deck. The air and sunshine did him good and soon he began to regain some of his old self-confidence — as long as the sea stayed calm.

Manuel Nicosa also was very useful and active. Juan de la Cosa taught him all he knew of navigation and before long he became an excellent sailing-master. His unfailing good spirits and his experience in handling men made him very popular with the sailors.

But by the first week in October everyone was beginning to be worried. For two months now we had sailed steadily west-

ward, yet there was still no sight of land. Day after day we sailed in the centre of a circle of empty horizon. Day after day the sun rose directly over our wake and set directly ahead. The pitch in the seams grew sticky with the heat, the great cloud castles piled up each afternoon, disappeared, and all was the same as before. Each day took us farther from the world we knew, and led us nowhere.

Food was running low, our wine was almost gone, even water was scarce. The crews were growing sullen, they no longer listened to Doña Mercedes' songs, they obeyed orders sluggishly.

It was about this time that I crushed a rebellion which might have been most disastrous. One night while perched in the rigging I became aware of a group of sailors muttering in the shadow of the mainmast.

Climbing softly down a stay I listened to their conversation and my blood ran cold as I realized what they were up to.

It was mutiny! Apparently they felt that Chris was a madman, that there was no land ahead, that we were doomed to sail on and on to some awful destruction. They were all armed with knives and handspikes and were even then on the point of attacking their officers, throwing their Admiral overboard and turning back toward Spain!

Hastily I flew down to the stern cabin to inform Nick and the Captain of our impending danger. Doña Mercedes turned pale, Chris pulled the covers over his head, but Manuel Nicosa quickly strapped on his great cavalry sabre while Juan de la Cosa picked up a cutlass. He was a giant of a man and his black beard bristled in anticipation of a fight.

"No, gentlemen, no," I said. "No bloodshed if we can avoid it. Leave this to Aurelio."

Flying silently up to the crosstrees, where I was completely hidden, I looked down upon the deck. I was just in time. The conspirators, in two groups, were advancing stealthily on the great stern cabin.

Taking a full breath I roared in a deep booming voice, "Throw down your arms! All is discovered!"

Wildly they stared in every direction, but could see no one. Again I boomed, "Throw them overboard, at once, or every man of you will hang from the yardarm at sunrise!"

At this moment Nick and Juan de la Cosa sauntered from the cabin. There was a series of splashes alongside as knives and handspikes were hastily thrown overboard.

Juan de la Cosa, treading catlike, advanced on the ringleader. Grasping him gently by the neck cloth he demanded: "What is all this hubbub? What were those splashes?"

"Nothing, my Captain, nothing at all," quaked the terrified seaman, "just fish, I am sure — just fish."

"Fish, ha, fish," De la Cosa murmured. "The poor fish must be hungry." Lifting him easily by the throat he moved toward the rail. "Shall we feed the poor fish?" he asked quietly. Then suddenly throwing the limp mutineer from him he roared, "Back to your kennel, dogs!"

The cowed sailors slunk forward, and our mutiny was over.

This one uprising was past, but all the men of the fleet were becoming restless and discouraged. Day after day I flew from ship to ship telling them about each hopeful sign. Evening after evening I encouraged them with talk of the gold and pearls to be found in my land, working myself to a skeleton.

But *I knew* that we were nearing the end of our voyage. The sea began to take on that glorious blue that exists only in the Caribbean. We plowed through league after league of Saragossa weed, familiar to me from childhood. The stars at night were becoming the stars I knew. And one morning the men sighted a great clumsy pelican flying out of the northwest.

I flew out and accompanied him for some distance. They are a stupid breed, the pelicans, and of course cannot talk; but I hastened back to the fleet and told the men that he had left the land only the day before, which encouraged them greatly.

And at night, as I perched on the mast-top, I could sometimes catch just the faintest trace of a scent of the jungle.

Then one glorious day, as I flew over to the *Pinta,* I spied something green floating in the water. Swooping down to investigate my heart gave a great bound, for it was a mango branch, with one mango still clinging to it! Shrieking with delight I carried it back to the *Santa María,* and shriveled and salty as it was I devoured every bit of it before speaking to any of the wondering crew.

"It's a mango, Chris!" I screamed. "Don't you understand? It's still fresh. We *can't* be far from land."

"*Land!*" murmured Chris, with closed eyes. "Land, oh land! If I ever set foot on land again I'll never set it off." Then he shouted: "Ten thousand maravedis and a silken cape to the first man who sights land!" He began to look green again and stumbled below to lie down.

That night as I perched on the mast-top I could smell jungle clearly! I could smell land!

Suddenly, far ahead where sky and sea met, I spied a tiny pinpoint of light. Springing into the air I flew toward it. In a few moments, I could see the faint outline of a sand beach. The light was a campfire around which a whole tribe of my dear Indians slumbered peacefully.

Oh, the delicious fragrance that rose from the treetops to welcome me! Oh, the soft warmth of the midnight air! I could have swooned for joy. But pausing only long enough to snatch one kumquat, I hastened back to the fleet.

Screaming raucously I circled the three ships. "Land Ho!" I shrieked, swooping down on the *Niña;* "Land! Land! Land ahead!" — as I passed over the *Pinta;* and, "Land, Chris, Land Ho! Land, Nick, Land!" I bawled, falling exhausted to the deck of the *Santa María.*

Bedlam broke loose through all the fleet. Cannon were fired, ship's bells rang. The sailors danced, embraced and whooped. Juan de la Cosa broke out the last barrel of wine. Doña Mercedes wept tears of joy.

In all this hubbub the only silent person was the Admiral of the Ocean Sea. At the first shout of "Land," he had turned greener than usual and flopped on the deck in a dead faint.

· 15 ·

THE GREAT

DISCOVERER

DAWN found the fleet anchored off a beautiful green island, but long before the anchors were dropped I had flown ashore.

How heavenly it was to be among treetops once more, what
joy to have ripe jungle fruit and a cool clear stream to bathe in!

I woke up the Indians, demanded *cracas* and plied them with questions. They were a tribe of fishermen, not very bright, but from them I learned that this was the Island of Guanahani, many many miles from my own land. Between here and the mainland, however, there were numerous islands by which I could fly home easily.

What a relief that was! "Almost home, at last," I said, and flew to a treetop to take a look at the fleet. It was long past sunup and although there were signs of activity on the ships no one had yet come ashore, so I flew out to the *Santa María*.

There all was confusion — and irritation. The sailors stood about in sullen groups. Juan de la Cosa plucked his beard and Nick paced the deck fuming with anger and heat.

"It's ridiculous, Aurelio," he burst out, "perfectly absurd. Here we've been cooped-up on these little ships for over two months and now we have to wait for hours while *he* arranges his silly costumes and 'appropriate ceremonies.' Who cares about ceremonies? I want a bath!"

At that moment Chris emerged from the cabin in the most gorgeous costume I had yet seen. Behind him came the Royal Historian, the Grand Constable, a few ship's boys bearing scrolls and banners, and several men-at-arms, sweating in their heavy armor. Solemnly they boarded the small boats and were rowed toward shore. I flew over and perched in a tree to watch the landing.

Chris stood proudly in the bow of the leading boat. As it approached the beach several sailors leaped into the water, pushed it well up on the sand, and the Admiral of the Ocean Sea stepped ashore, the first white man to set foot in the New World!

The cannon of the fleet boomed, the musicians trumpeted and the terrified Indians all fled hastily into the forest. While the sailors prayed and sang Te Deums, Chris stuck his sword into the sand and in a loud voice took possession of this land in the name of Their Royal Majesties, Ferdinand and Isabella of Spain.

The men were frantic to explore the forests, gather fruit and swim in the crystal clear surf, but Chris kept them all standing stiffly at attention while he read a seemingly endless speech.

A tall cross was then set up in the sand, the great banners of León, Castile and Aragon were planted near it, the sailors erected a wooden framework over which a crimson silk canopy was stretched and an ornate chair was placed beneath it for the Admiral.

A large number of baskets and a set of scales were brought; then Chris, after seating himself, grandly motioned the Captains to step up for their orders.

"Your men will now gather the gold and pearls," he said; "and be sure that every bit is brought here to me. The Grand Constable will weigh all treasure and the Royal Historian will keep a careful account, paying especial attention to my one-eighth share.

"You may inform the native rulers that the Admiral of the Ocean Sea will now be pleased to receive them."

Bored by all this rigmarole, I dozed off and did not wake for several hours. When I did I ate a few kumquats and strolled down to the beach.

The sailors were like boys suddenly released from school. They were bathing and shouting in the surf, washing clothes, gathering fruit, laughing and trying to talk to the shy, friendly Indians.

Chris, however, was in no such pleasant mood. Under the red velvet canopy he sat, sweltering in his fur-edged Admiral's cloak, while two sullen men-at-arms stood at attention on either side of him. Sitting stiffly in the uncomfortable chair he looked a little like Isabella granting an audience. But the only audience here was a few sea gulls and two Indian chiefs who squatted in the sand and laughingly tried to answer his questions. The treasure baskets were empty, the Royal Historian dozed over his blank lists.

Before I could speak Chris demanded with a glare, "Why were you absent from the Landing Ceremonies? How dared you go ashore before the Admiral of the Ocean Sea?"

"Why Chris," I said, "I didn't know — "

"You will address me as 'Your Excellency,' " he said harshly. "As Governor General of these lands I hold power of life and death over every living being here. This includes Indians — and parrots. One more bit of insolence and I will have you put in chains!"

I could scarcely believe my ears. "Put me in chains? *Me?* Why, Chris, the sun must have affected you!"

"I will also tolerate no more deceit or treachery," he shouted. "Where are the gold and silver? Where are the pearls? You claimed that you had taught me to speak Indian, and these giggling idiots cannot understand a word I say. They have no gold, they haven't even got clothes!"

I was bewildered by his tone — and becoming annoyed.

"Now listen to me, Your Excellent Excellency, or whatever you call yourself," I shouted back. "There is no treasure here because you have not yet reached the gold country. I could have told you that. This little island has no treasure. These Indians are simple fishermen who don't talk the dialect I taught you.

They are not interested in gold or silver — or you either, except as something to laugh at. The gold lies four or five hundred miles farther west, and it's a good rough bit of ocean. I hope you enjoy it."

I stamped off in a rage and found Nick and Doña Mercedes bathing in a brook back in the jungle.

"Oh, Aurelio," cried Doña Mercedes. "Where have you been and *what* has come over Don Cristóbal? The moment he stepped on dry land and forgot his seasickness he became simply impossible. Such airs and graces! Such pomp and ceremony! Why, I think the man is mad!"

"*Think!*" I snorted, "I've always known it." I then explained where we were and where the gold country lay. "But he'll never sail there," I said. "*He'll* not go a mile farther if he can help it."

"Poor Aurelio," said Doña Mercedes. "You have made this whole expedition possible, you have worked *so* hard just to get home — and you're not there yet."

"Oh, that's all right," I answered. "There's a whole string of islands between here and my home. I can fly it easily. What worries me is that I promised you and Nick bushels of gold and a hatful of pearls. Well, at least I can give you the ten thousand maravedis and the silk cloak that I earned by being the first to sight land, that's something."

But even this pleasure was denied me. For when we returned to the beach and I demanded my reward Chris laughed in my face.

"The reward," he sneered unpleasantly, "was offered to the first *man* who discovered land. Do you consider yourself a man? Ridiculous! The reward goes to *me*, Don Cristóbal Colón, Admiral of the Ocean Sea; Don Cristóbal, the Great Commander."

I had put up with his pompous pretensions for a long time but this was the last straw. Flying to a safe branch I unburdened my mind.

"Admiral Seasick!" I jeered. "The Great Commander indeed! Who told you about this land in the first place? I did. Who got you an audience at Court? I did. Who had you

made an Admiral? I did. Who raised the money for this 'Glorious Venture'? I did. Who sighted land first? I did; I, Aurelio.

"Well, here you are, on a small island, with no gold, no silver and no pearls. You're afraid to go on and afraid to go back. As far as I'm concerned you can stay here and swelter under your crimson canopy for the rest of your life. *I'm through.* I'm going home. *I* don't have to go back empty-handed and face Ferdinand or Isabella — or Torquemada! Now let's see what you can do without Aurelio. Now put me in chains!" And I flew off into the jungle.

Flying by easy stages from island to island, I reached my home in a few days.

What a welcome I had! Friends and relations gathered from near and far, and I had to tell the story of my wanderings a thousand times. When not talking I ate fruit; it seemed as though I could never get enough.

But after a couple of months of this jollity and feasting, I began to feel a little guilty about Nick and Doña Mercedes. After all, I *had* promised them gold and pearls; and I had also promised that they would get back to Spain.

So I gathered, from various Indian acquaintances, a sack of enormous pearls and a few gold nuggets. Then, with a group of my friends who were eager to see the great ships I had talked so much about, I flew back to Guanahani to learn how the "Great Adventure" was faring.

The Expedition was still there, but the *Santa María* lay wrecked on a sand bar. The beach was befouled with burned-out campfires and litter. All the Indians seemed to have fled into the jungle. I located Nick and Doña Mercedes at their favorite swimming place.

"Aurelio!" she cried, clasping me tight. "Our darling Aurelio, you've come back to us!"

"Not for long," I said. "How are you, and how's the Expedition?"

"Terrible," said Nick, "perfectly terrible. Don Cristóbal gets more erratic every day. He let the *Santa María* get wrecked on a sand bar and he just sits under his velvet canopy dressed up in his Admiral's robes all day long, while the mosquitoes and sand fleas bite him.

"For three whole months now we've waited here while he's tried to decide whether to go on or go back. All the treasure he's found is about a handful of gold and a few Indian arrowheads. I suppose we'll just sit here for the rest of our lives, and me with a horse and a Colonel's Commission waiting in Spain."

Doña Mercedes seemed on the point of tears. "Oh, Aurelio," she said plaintively, "I do *so* want to go home. Do you remember how homesick you were in Spain? I feel just like that now. I want to go home!"

"All right, children, all right," I said. "Old Aurelio the Great Arranger will just have to get to work again. Cheer up now, while I go and try to make up his mind for him. And by the way, here's a little something to start housekeeping on," and I tossed them the bag of pearls.

"But Aurelio," cried Doña Mercedes, in astonishment. "These are priceless! They are worth fortunes! We can't accept them."

"You might as well," I said. "They're no use to me. I don't play marbles. But don't let *him* see them, he'll claim his eighth part — or more."

I found Chris still sitting under his canopy, which was quite faded by now. He looked faded too, very thin and insect-bitten.

The treasure baskets were still there and still empty. I really felt sorry for him — almost.

"Well Chris, you haven't done so well without Aurelio, have you?" I asked not very unkindly.

He was almost too crushed to answer.

"Oh, Aurelio, it's awful," he sighed. "I just can't go on any farther, you know my weakness; and I daren't go back empty-handed. All night I lie awake thinking of Torquemada. What shall I say to Isabella, what will Ferdinand call me?"

"If you work things right," I said, "he'll call you the GREAT DISCOVERER. Now listen, Chris, just forget about the treasure. Here's a bag of gold nuggets. Give them to Isabella and tell her they're only a sample.

"But what you *must* do is to tell them you've discovered a New World. Tell them you've discovered AMERICA! Take back a lot of plants; sweet potatoes and tobacco and things like that. Take birds and animals, take fruits and flowers, take a few Indians. Tell them you've found the greatest, richest, most fertile land in all the world!

"Why, they'll make a hero of you. They'll call it the greatest discovery of all time. There will be monuments to you all over the world. There'll be cities and streets and even holidays named after you!"

As I talked I could see him cheering up. I could see that he was already planning new costumes and decorations.

"Perhaps you're right, Aurelio," he said finally, "you always seem to be right. Would you suggest green or orange for the Great Discoverer's cape?"

Two days later the Expedition, what was left of it, sailed for Spain. My friends and I circled the *Niña* and the *Pinta* calling good-bys to all my old shipmates, Juan de la Cosa, Martin Alonzo Pinzon and the rest. Doña Mercedes waved happily.

But of Chris there was no sign. Manuel Nicosa made a derisive gesture and pointed toward the cabin.

"Admiral of the Ocean Sea!" he jeered. "The Great Discoverer — Pooh!"

As we watched them sail away into the rising sun one of my companions asked, "I wonder if he'll ever come back again and really discover something?"

"I wouldn't be surprised," I said, selecting a juicy mango. "I think he will if Isabella can persuade him, and she's quite a persuader, is Isabella."

THE END

DO NOT RETURN IN JIFFY BAG